OTTER ON HIS OWN
The Story of a Sea Otter

SMITHSONIAN OCEANIC COLLECTION

For my father and mother, who share my love for the sea — D.B.

To my three loves: Judy, Mike, & James — R.L.

Text copyright © 2002 Doe Boyle.
Illustrations copyright © 2002 Robert Lawson.
Book copyright © 2002 Trudy Corporation and the Smithsonian Institution, Washington DC 20560.

Published by Soundprints Division of Trudy Corporation, Norwalk, Connecticut.

Series design, book layout: Shields & Partners
Editor: Laura Gates Galvin

First Edition 1995
Second Edition 2002
10 9 8 7 6 5 4 3 2 1
Printed in Singapore

Acknowledgments:
    Our very special thanks to Dr. Don E. Wilson of the Department of Systematic Biology at
the Smithsonian Institution's National Museum of Natural History for his curatorial review.
    Soundprints would also like to thank Ellen Nanney and Robyn Bissette at the Smithsonian
Institution's Office of Product Development and Licensing for their help in the creation of this book.
    The author thanks the following individuals for their input: Ellen Faurot-Daniels, Dina Stansbury and
Susan Brown from Friends of the Sea Otter in Carmel, California; LeAnn Gast and Dennis Maroulas from
the Aquarium for Wildlife Conservation in New York City; and Daniel, Spanky, Elsa and Bunky, a "raft"
of southern sea otters rehabilitated at Monterey Bay Aquarium and now residents of Coney Island, New York.

Library of Congress Cataloging-in-Publication Data

Boyle, Doe.
  Otter on his own : the story of a sea otter / by Doe Boyle ; illustrated by Robert Lawson.
        p.   cm.
  Summary: Otter Pup spends the first months of his life with his mother in a protected cove off the coast of
California, learning how to hunt for food and care for himself.
  ISBN 1-56899-129-0 — ISBN 1-56899-130-4 (micro hardcover)
1. Sea otter—Juvenile fiction. [1. Sea otter—Fiction. 2. Otters—Fiction.] I. Lawson, Robert, 1955- ill. II. Title.

PZ10.3.B715 Ot 2002
[E]—dc21

2001049690

OTTER ON HIS OWN
The Story of a Sea Otter

by Doe Boyle   Illustrated by Robert Lawson

Soundprints
Where Children Discover...

In a sheltered cove at the edge of the Pacific Ocean, a sea otter pup and his mother lie cradled in a golden-brown bed of giant kelp. A foghorn echoes from the rocky point as the morning mist rises.

Like a woolly ball, Otter Pup rests on his mother's chest. He is two hours old, and today is his first day on the sea.

The sunshine of late winter warms the rocky California shore, but the water is cold. Otter Pup's loose fur protects him like cozy pajamas. His mother keeps his fur clean and dry by rubbing it between her forepaws and blowing warm air into it with her mouth and nose.

Otter Pup's mother is hungry. She plucks Otter Pup from her belly and plops him on the surface of the sea. She drapes a smooth ribbon of kelp across his belly to anchor him. Otter Pup bobs up and down on the waves like a cork while his mother dives below to forage for her dinner.

Otter Pup shrieks for his missing mother. He hears only the sounds of the other pups and mothers in the cove.

Otter Pup barks and splashes. Finally, his mother pops up from under the water. She coos at Otter Pup and props him up on her belly. Otter Pup watches as his mother pulls the soft meat from a sea urchin she has found in the forest of kelp.

When she is finished eating, Otter Pup's mother rolls and tumbles in the water to clean her fur. Otter Pup tries to tumble with her, but he is too young. He calls to his twirling mother with a piercing wail, and she comes to play with him in the waves.

For several months, Otter Pup shares his mother's food. Otter Pup's mother breaks the hard shells of clams, abalone, and urchins on rocks she finds on the ocean floor.

Crack! Crack! The sound of her pounding carries above the cries of the hovering gulls who wait to steal fallen morsels.

By springtime, Otter Pup is sleek and strong. He can swim and somersault like his mother. He is eager to search the world beneath the waves for his own dinner. It is time for his first dive.

With a great who-oo-sh of bubbles, Otter Pup rolls forward and pushes downward with his webbed hind feet.

Otter Pup has not pushed hard enough. He grabs a frond of kelp to pull himself all the way to the sandy bottom.

Snails and mussels and darting fish are everywhere. Otter Pup sees crabs and limpets and sea stars—all for the choosing! Even small octopuses hide in the rusting cans caught among the rocks.

Otter Pup's mother dives for her dinner, too. Watching her, Otter Pup tucks snails and clams into the loose folds of fur under his forelegs.

Finally, Otter Pup and his mother grab urchins in their forepaws, then swim to the top of the kelp to enjoy their feast.

Floating on his back, Otter Pup spreads his dinner on his belly and tears at an urchin. He snorts and sniffs, plucking snail treasure from his "pocket." Sometimes he picks out pebbles he has taken by mistake.

Throughout the warm days of spring, Otter Pup perfects his hunting and diving. He learns to pry the stubborn abalone from the rocks below. After each dive and every meal, he grooms himself carefully. Bits of his food or oil from the huge ships that pass offshore can mat his thick fur. He keeps each hair spotlessly clean.

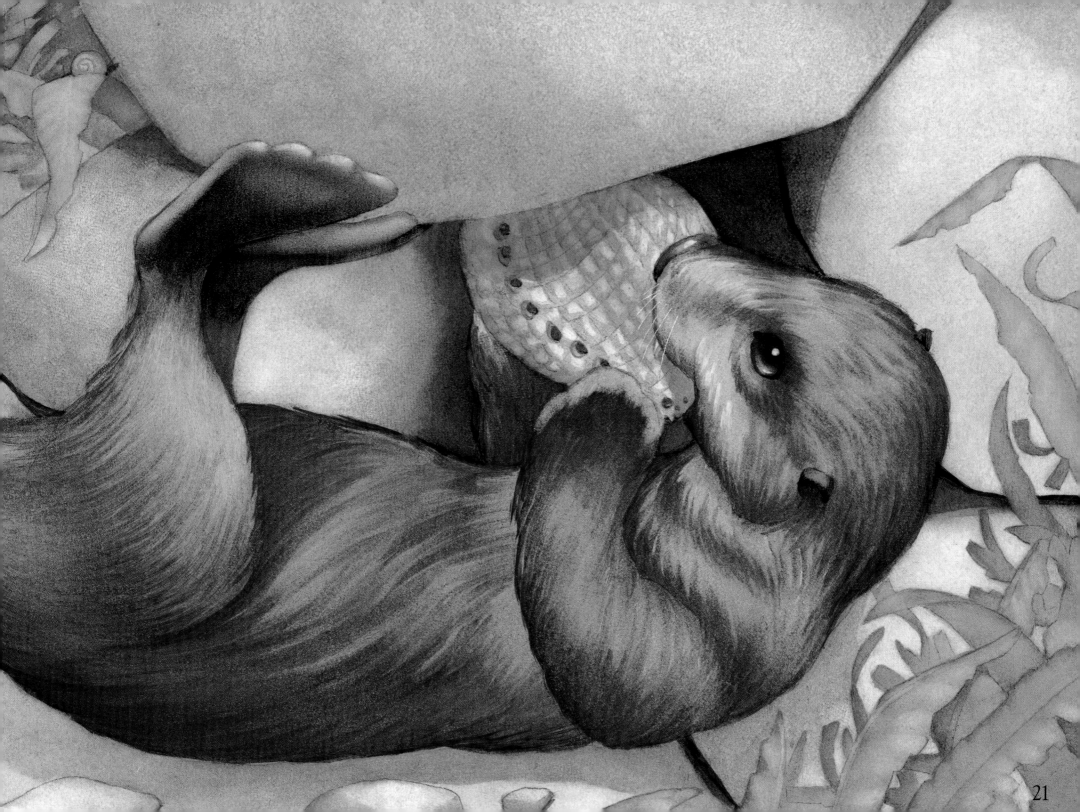

One afternoon Otter Pup's mother leaves the cove to look for squid. Otter Pup is curious. Following her beyond the rocky point, Otter Pup feels the powerful breath of the ocean on his whiskers. Under the choppy swells, Otter Pup hears new sounds—the chirps and whistles of dolphins, the whir and thunder of boats. He cannot hear or see his mother.

Otter Pup calls, but his mother does not answer. A silent creature streaks by him. His heart pounds as he spots his mother in the path of the great white shark. With a tremendous shake, the shark hurls Otter Pup's mother high above the salty spray. Screaming, she slams down into the water and disappears.

Otter Pup cries and frantically searches the water for his mother. He feels a rough tug at his forepaw. He whirls about, but the vicious shark is gone, searching for tastier prey. It is his mother who is at his side, pushing him toward the safety of the kelp.

They race forward until the gentle kelp encircles them. Tonight there will be no diving. Rocking side by side, Otter Pup and his mother sleep.

At dawn, the cove is foggy and quiet, except for the bellow of the foghorn. Otter Pup's mother is bruised and feeds lazily on the snails in the kelp canopy, while Otter Pup dives alone for the sweet, pink flesh of abalone.

By summer's end, Otter Pup is almost fully grown. The world beyond the cove is full of danger, but he is filled with a new curiosity and restlessness.

One morning Otter Pup leaves his mother. He swims out past the rocky point, out past the foghorn.

Today is Otter's first day on his own.

About the Sea Otter

One of the smallest marine mammals, sea otters live close to the Pacific coast in waters about 30 to 50 feet deep. Sea otter pups usually stay with their mothers for six to nine months, often with other otters in a group called a raft. Sea otters have the densest fur of any creature on earth, with up to a million hairs per square inch. This hair traps air bubbles, insulating them against the cold water.

Sea otters eat many invertebrates, which are animals without backbones. Among them are abalone, whose shells sea otters crack open with rocks. This behavior makes sea otters one of the few tool-using animals. They are also able to pry open submerged cans with their teeth to eat the young octopuses that live inside.

Sea otters came close to extinction during The Great Hunt that began in 1743. In 1911, they gained protection under a law that prohibited otter hunting and the sale of otter pelts. Even though sea otters have increased in numbers, hazards created by humans keep their survival in question.

Glossary

abalone: A rock-hugging mollusk that clings to surfaces with a large, muscular "foot."

giant kelp: A fast-growing greenish-brown seaweed that flourishes along the California coast. Kelp forests attach to rocks on the sea bottom and grow to the surface, forming beds. Their long branches, or fronds, are kept afloat by small balloon-like bladders.

limpet: A mollusk with a conical shell that clings tightly to rocks.

sea urchin: A round invertebrate with a thin, brittle shell covered with movable spines.

squid: A marine animal with a long tapered body and ten arms.

webbed: Having skin between the fingers or toes for extra swimming power.

Points of Interest in this Book

pp. 4-5: giant kelp; lighthouse.
pp. 10-11: sea urchin.
pp. 12-13: seagulls; clams.
pp. 16-17: sea star; limpet (on rock at upper center); mussels (on rock at center right); octopus; crab; sea snail (on rock at far right).

pp. 20-21: abalone.
pp. 22-23: dolphins; steam ship.
pp. 24-25: great white shark.